Dear Cataleine
I love
this book!
Hope you do.

P.S. a true story

love Judee

11/18/00

Thank you,
Mr. Falker

PATRICIA POLACCO

Thank you, Mr. Falker

PHILOMEL BOOKS   NEW YORK

Patricia Lee Gauch, Editor.

Copyright © 1998 by Patricia Polacco

All rights reserved. This book, or parts thereof, may not be reproduced

in any form without permission in writing from the publisher, Philomel Books,

a division of The Putnam & Grosset Group, 200 Madison Avenue, New York, NY 10016.

Philomel Books, Reg. U.S. Pat, & Tm. Off. Published simultaneously in Canada.

Printed in Hong Kong by South China Printing Co. (1988) Ltd.

Book designed by Donna Mark. Text set in Garth Graphic.

Library of Congress Cataloging-in-Publication Data

Polacco, Patricia. Thank you, Mr. Falker / Patricia Polacco. p. cm.

Summary: At first, Trisha loves school, but her difficulty learning to read makes

her feel dumb, until, in the fifth grade, a new teacher helps her understand

and overcome her problem. [1. Reading—Fiction. 2. Teachers—Fiction.]

I. Title. PZ7.P75186Tf 1998 [E]—DC21 97-18685 CIP AC

ISBN 0-399-23166-8

3 5 7 9 10 8 6 4 2

To George Felker, the real Mr. Falker.
You will forever be my hero.

The grandpa held the jar of honey so that all the family could see, then dipped a ladle into it and drizzled honey on the cover of a small book.

The little girl had just turned five.

"Stand up, little one," he cooed. "I did this for your mother, your uncles, your older brother, and now you!"

Then he handed the book to her. "Taste!"

She dipped her finger into the honey and put it into her mouth.

"What is that taste?" the grandma asked.

The little girl answered, "Sweet!"

Then all of the family said in a single voice, "Yes, and so is knowledge, but knowledge is like the bee that made that sweet honey, you have to chase it through the pages of a book!"

The little girl knew that the promise to read was at last hers. Soon she was going to learn to read.

Trisha, the littlest girl in the family, grew up loving books. Her schoolteacher mother read to her every night. Her redheaded brother brought his books home from school and shared them. And whenever she visited the family farm, her grandfather or grandmother read to her by the stone fireplace.

When she turned five and went to kindergarten, most of all she hoped to read. Each day she saw the kids in the first grade across the hall reading, and before the year was over, some of the kids in her own class began to read. Not Trisha.

Still, she loved being at school because she could draw. The other kids would crowd around her and watch her do her magic with the crayons.

"In first grade, you'll learn to read," her brother said.

In first grade, Trisha sat in a circle with the other kids. They were all holding *Our Neighborhood*, their first reader, sounding out letters and words. They said, "Beh, beh . . . oy, boy, and luh, luh . . . ook, look." The teacher smiled at them when they put all the sounds together and got a word right.

But when Trisha looked at a page, all she saw were wiggling shapes, and when she tried to sound out words, the other kids laughed at her.

"Trisha, what are you looking at in that book?" they'd say.

"I'm reading!" she'd say back to them.

But her teacher would move on to the next person. Always when it was her turn to read, her teacher had to help her with every single word. And while the other kids moved up into the second reader and third reader, she stayed alone in *Our Neighborhood*.

Trisha began to feel "different." She began to feel dumb.

The harder words got for the little girl, the more and more time she spent drawing—how she loved to draw!—or just sitting and dreaming. Or, when she could, going for walks with her grandmother.

One summer day she and her grandma were walking together in the small woods behind their farm. It was twilight. The air was sweet and warm. Fireflies were just coming up from the grasses.

As they walked, Trisha said, "Gramma, do you think I'm . . . different?"

"Of course," her grandma answered. "To be different is the miracle of life. You see all of those little fireflies? Every one is different."

"Do you think I'm smart?" Trisha didn't feel smart.

Her grandma hugged her. "You are the smartest, quickest, dearest little thing ever."

Right then the little girl felt safe in her grandma's arms. Reading didn't matter so much.

Trisha's grandma used to say that the stars were holes in the sky. They were the light of heaven coming from the other side. And she used to say that someday she would be on the other side, where the light comes from.

One evening they lay on the grass together and counted the lights from heaven. "You know," her grandma said, "all of us will go there someday. Hang on to the grass, or you'll lift right off the ground, and there you'll be!"

They laughed, and both hung on to the grass.

But it was not long after that night that her grandma must have let go of the grass, because she went to where the lights were, on the other side. And not long after that, Trisha's grandpa let go of the grass, too.

School seemed harder and harder now.

Reading was just plain torture. When Sue Ellyn read her page, or Tommy Bob read his page, they read so easily that Trisha would watch the top of their heads to see if something was happening to their heads that wasn't happening to hers.

And numbers were the hardest thing of all to read. She never added anything right.

"Line the numbers up before you add them," the teacher would say. But when Trisha tried, the numbers looked like a stack of blocks, wobbly and ready to fall.

She just knew she was dumb.

Then, one day, her mother announced that she had gotten a teaching job in California! A long way from the family farm in Michigan.

Even though her grandma and grandpa were gone, the little girl didn't want to move. Maybe, though, the teachers and kids in her new school wouldn't know how dumb she was.

She and her mother and brother moved across the country in a two-tone l949 Plymouth. It took five days.

But at the new school it was the same. When she tried to read, she stumbled over words: "the cah, cah. . .cat. . .rrrr, rrr. . .ran." She was reading like a baby in the third grade!

And when her teacher read along with them, and called on Trisha for an answer, she gave the wrong answer every time.

"Hey, dummy!" a boy called out to her on the playground, "How come you are so dumb?" Other kids stood near him and they laughed.

Trisha could feel the tears burning in her eyes. How she longed to go back to her grandparents' farm in Michigan.

Now Trisha wanted to go to school less and less. "I have a sore throat," she'd say to her mother. Or, "I have a stomachache." She dreamed more and more, and drew more and more, and she hated, hated, hated school.

Then, when Trisha started fifth grade, the school was all abuzz. There was a new teacher. He was tall and elegant. Everybody loved his striped coat and slick gray pants—he wore the neatest clothes.

All the usual teacher's pets gathered around him—Stevie Joe and Alice Marie, Davy and Michael Lee. But right from the start, it didn't seem to matter to Mr. Falker which kids were the cutest. Or the smartest. Or the best at anything.

Mr. Falker would stand behind Trisha whenever she was drawing, and whisper, "This is brilliant . . . absolutely brilliant. Do you know how talented you are?"

When he said this, even the kids who teased her would turn around in their seats and look at her drawings. But they still laughed whenever she gave a wrong answer.

Then, one day, she had to stand up and read, which she hated. She was stumbling through a page in *Charlotte's Web*, and the page was going all fuzzy, when the kids began to laugh out loud.

Mr. Falker, in his plaid jacket and his butterfly tie, said, "Stop! Are all of you so perfect that you can look at another person and find fault with her?"

That was the last day anyone laughed out loud. Or made fun of her. All except Eric. He had sat behind Trisha for two whole years, but he seemed almost to hate her. Trisha didn't know why.

He waited by the door of the classroom for her and pulled her hair. He waited for her on the playground, leaned in her face, and called her, "Toad!"

Trisha was afraid to turn any corner, for fear Eric would be there. She felt completely alone.

The only time she was really happy was when she was around Mr. Falker. He let her erase the blackboards—only the best students got to do that. He patted her on the back whenever she got something right, and he looked hard and mean at any kid who teased her.

You don't count
NO HOPER
stupid
toad!
hey dummy
You're ugly!
dummie
dummy!
stupid
You don't belong
not one of us
UGLY
stupid

But the nicer Mr. Falker was to Trisha, the worse Eric treated her. He got all the other kids to wait for her on the playground, or in the cafeteria, or even in the bathroom, and to jump out and call her "Stupid!" or "Ugly!"

And Trisha began to believe them.

She discovered that if she asked to go to the bathroom just before recess, she could hide under the inside stairwell during the free time, and not have to go outside at all. In that dark place she felt completely safe.

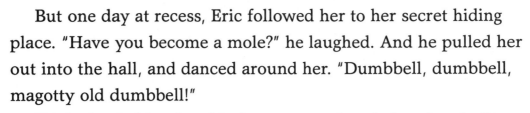

But one day at recess, Eric followed her to her secret hiding place. "Have you become a mole?" he laughed. And he pulled her out into the hall, and danced around her. "Dumbbell, dumbbell, magotty old dumbbell!"

Trisha buried her head in her arms and curled up in a ball. Suddenly, she heard footsteps. It was Mr. Falker.

He marched Eric down to the office. When he came back, he found Trisha. "I don't think you'll have to worry about that boy again," he said softly.

"What was he teasing you about, little one?"

"I don't know." Trisha shrugged.

Trisha was sure Mr. Falker believed that she could read. She had learned to memorize what the kid next to her was reading. Or she would wait for Mr. Falker to help her with a sentence, then she'd say the same thing that he did. "Good," he would say.

Then, one day, Mr. Falker asked her to stay after school and help wash the blackboards. He put on music and brought out little sandwiches as they worked and talked.

All at once he said, "Let's play a game! I'll shout out letters. You write them on the board with the wet sponge as quickly as you can."

"A," he shouted. She wiped a watery A.

"Eight," he shouted. She made a watery 8.

"Fourteen...Three...D...M...Q," he shouted out. He shouted out many, many letters and numbers. Then he walked up behind her, and together they looked at the board.

It was a watery mess. Trisha knew that none of the letters or numbers looked like they should. She threw the sponge down and tried to run.

But Mr. Falker caught her arm and sank to his knees in front of her. "You poor baby," he said. "You think you're dumb, don't you? How awful for you to be so lonely and afraid."

She sobbed.

"But, little one, don't you understand, you don't see letters or numbers the way other people do. And you've gotten through school all this time, and fooled many, many good teachers!" He smiled at her. "That took cunning, and smartness, and such, such bravery."

Then he stood up and finished washing the board. "We're going to change all that, girl. You're going to read—I promise you that."

Now, almost every day after school, she met with Mr. Falker and Miss Plessy, a reading teacher. They did a lot of things she didn't even understand! At first she made circles in sand, and then big sponge circles on the blackboard, going from left to right, left to right.

Another day they flicked letters on a screen, and Trisha shouted them out loud. Still other days she worked with wooden blocks and built words. Letters, letters, letters. Words, words, words. Always sounding them out. And that felt good.

But, though she'd read words, she hadn't read a whole sentence. And deep down she still felt dumb.

And then one spring day—had it been three months or four months since they had started?—Mr. Falker put a book in front of her. She'd never seen it before. He picked a paragraph in the middle of a page and pointed at it.

Almost as if it were magic, or as if light poured into her brain, the words and sentences started to take shape on the page as they never had before. "She...marched...them...off...to..." Slowly, she read a sentence. Then another, and another. And finally she'd read a paragraph. And she understood the whole thing.

She didn't notice that Mr. Falker and Miss Plessy had tears in their eyes.

That night, Trisha ran home without stopping to catch her breath. She bounded up the front steps, threw open her front door, and ran through the dining room to the kitchen. She climbed up on the cupboard and grabbed a jar of honey.

Then she went into the living room and found the book on a shelf, the very book that her grandpa had shown her so many years ago. She spooned honey on the cover and tasted the sweetness, and said to herself, "The honey is sweet, and so is knowledge, but knowledge is like the bee who made the honey, it has to be chased through the pages of a book!"

Then she held the book, honey and all, close to her chest. She could feel tears roll down her cheeks, but they weren't tears of sadness—she was happy, so very happy.

The rest of the year became an odyssey of discovery and adventure for the little girl. She learned to love school. I know because that little girl was me, Patricia Polacco.

I saw Mr. Falker again some thirty years later at a wedding. I walked up to him and introduced myself. At first he had difficulty placing me. Then I told him who I was, and how he had changed my life so many years ago.

He hugged me and asked me what I did for a living. "Why, Mr. Falker," I answered. "I make books for children. . . . Thank you, Mr. Falker. Thank you."